Her Majesty's Explorer:
a Steampunk bedtime story

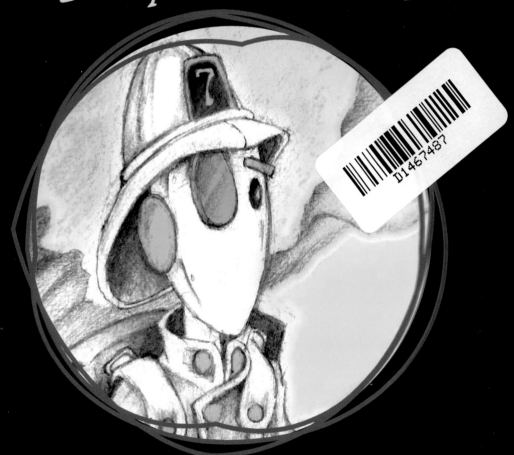

Written by
Emilie P. Bush

Illustrated by
William Kevin Petty

Dedications:

To my little explorers, Eleanor and Saralyn. ~E.P.B.

To soldiers, who are my friends and family. ~ W.K.P

Her Majesty's Explorer: a Steampunk bedtime story

Written by Emilie P. Bush

Illustrated by William Kevin Petty

Layout Design and Color by Theresa MeiHwa Curtis

Cover: illustrated by William Kevin Petty,

watercolor by Bridie Rollins,

a watercolor artist who lives and paints in Louisiana.

ISBN-13: 978-0984902804

ISBN-10: 0984902805

St. John Murphy Alexander,

a young automaton,

rested,

polished,

clean

and

fresh,

set out to march
at dawn.

He scouted
through
the dusty hills,
on hard
and
crusty plains,

Traversing rivers, dry ravines,
through blazing sun and rain.

alone and quiet,

observing all he passed.

Then home
to his regiment,

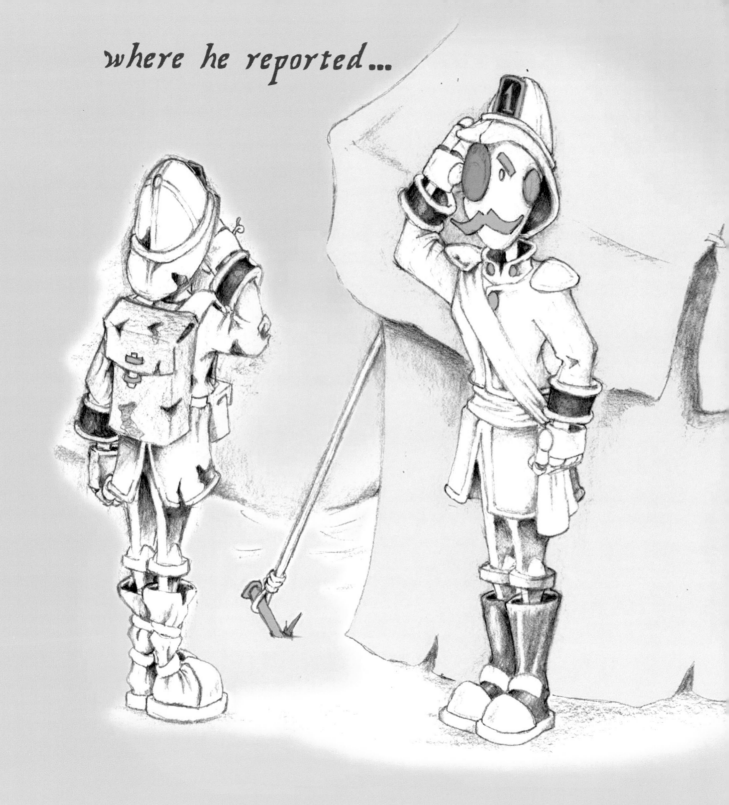

then collapsed.

His cogs were gummed, his gizmos gunked, his joints were caked with goo.

St. John took the doc's commands
and stumbled toward the mess

For a sip of oil and nosh of grease -
to sate him (more or less).

Stars lit the path
as St.John trudged
the distance to
his billet.

He dumped pebbles
from each boot,

and his boiler
– he did fill it.

The bed invited,
warm and soft,
to jump in
he was tempted,

But rules and
regulations said
no sleep until
he tended
to the cleaning
of his kit,
his feet
and uniform,

TAKE CARE
OF YOUR KIT.
AND YOUR KIT W
TAKE CARE OF YO

So, he stored his pack,
   sprayed his toes,
and sewed up
   what was torn.

He stitched a button on his shirt,
and deftly shined
each boot.

He swabbed away
the dust and grime,
he sat alone and mute.

When clothes and gear
were set to right,
then St. John groomed
his tin.

He wiped his eyes,
unscrewed his ears
and found
a bug within.

He brushed the grime from
'round his mouth
and filled a
water tub.

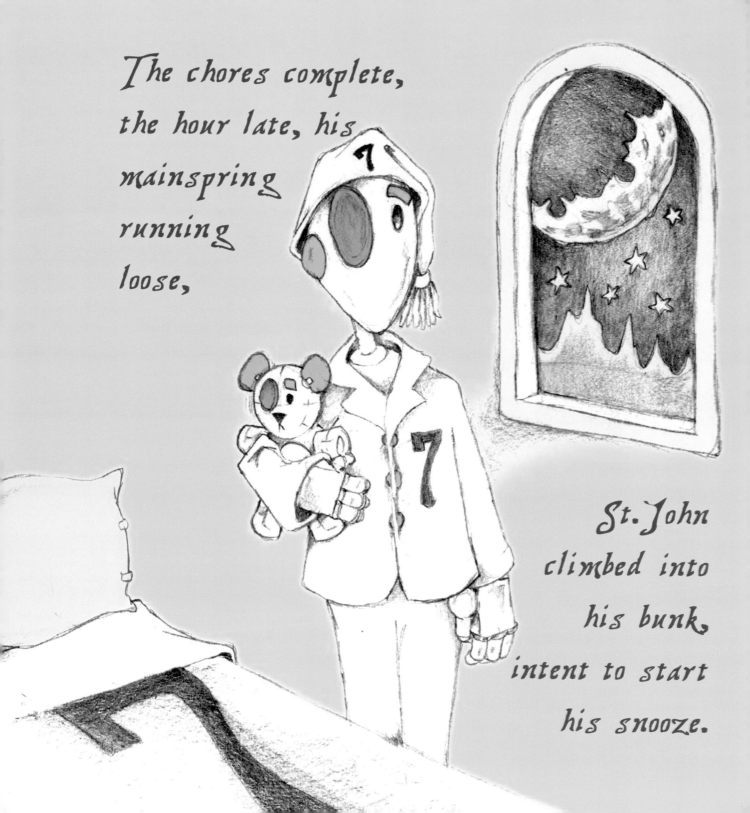

The chores complete,
the hour late, his
mainspring
running
loose,

St. John
climbed into
his bunk,
intent to start
his snooze.

He sighed
and shuddered
and ground to sleep,
where marching filled his dreams
with dusty hills, fields of flowers
and bubbly swollen streams.

When morning comes,
St. John will rise
and once again
be keen
to go exploring
near and far
for country,
cause and queen.

Foot soldier
of the regiment,

Explorer
meant to wander,

Automaton
of Her Majesty,

St. John
Murphy
Alexander.

THREE CHEERS

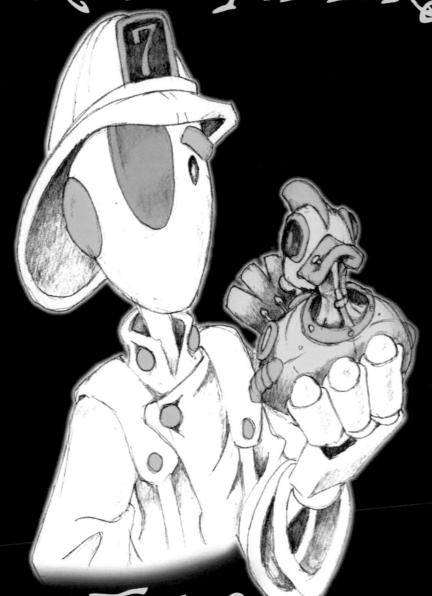

FOR STEAMDUCK

Steamduck flicks his clockwork tail,

In your bath is where he'll sail,

His smokestack leaves a wispy trail,

SOAP

— give three cheers for Steamduck!

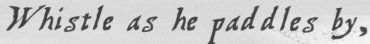

Whistle as he paddles by,

Try your best
to meet his eye,

You won't sink him,
but you can try,

— a mechanical wonder, Steamduck!

Made of gears and fit with cogs,
Exploring rivers, streams
and bogs,
A pal to
otters,
fish
and frogs,

— a friend to all, dear Steamduck.

Invented in a tinker's shop,
His motion fueled by soda pop,
Never will our hero stop,
— he'll swim forever, Steamduck.

Tell your friends and tell your mother,

You saw a duckie like no other,

A sight
to fill your
life with wonder,

— the one and only Steamduck.

Seek And Find

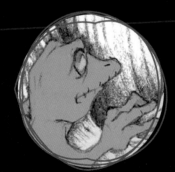

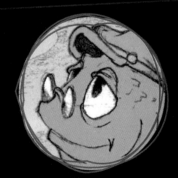

About the Author: Journalist and writer Emilie P. Bush has written two novels. Her first, Chenda and the Airship Brofman, was a "ripping good yarn!" and the tale was a 2010 Semi-finalist for the Amazon Breakthrough Novel Award. The Gospel According to Verdu picks up the epic tale where Chenda left off - high in the skies. Emilie P. Bush lives, laughs and writes with her family in Atlanta.

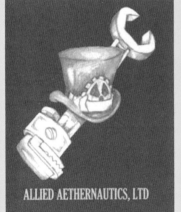

About the Illustrator: William Kevin Petty is the founder of Allied Aethernautics, LTD., a Steampunk illustration company and specializes in exceptionally detailed pencil sketches and and acrylic paintings. His work has appeared in Steampunk Magazine and across the web. Capt. Petty, when he is not deployed with the U.S. Army, lives and draws in central Louisiana.

Acknowledgments : Special thanks go to Bridie Rollins for the watercolor addition to W.K.P's cover illustration. Mrs. Rollins is an Artist-in-Residence at River Oaks Square Arts Center in Alexandria, Louisiana. She is an active member of Louisiana Watercolor Society, and her work is collected internationally.

About the Layout Designer: Theresa MeiHwa Curtis's creative talents can be found in the art and pre-press fields doing color-work, commercial and packaging layout design and web creation. A passionate children's story collector, she jumped at the chance to design H.M.E., her first picture book. Mrs. Curtis's family and her friends in the Atlanta Steampunk Community enjoy her exquisite costume design and tailoring.

13958704R00020

Made in the USA
Lexington, KY
29 February 2012